Something Soon

The Journey to the Start

Table of Contents

CHAPTER ONE 1

CHAPTER TWO... 11

CHAPTER THREE.. 29

CHAPTER FOUR... 49

CHAPTER FIVE..71

CHAPTER SIX 85

CHAPTER SEVEN 97

CHAPTER ONE

Seditionists HQ

Los Angeles

Daven sat back in his chair and tented his fingers thoughtfully. The dreaded first contact had gone exactly as badly as he expected, but now all he could do about the Bancroft boys was wait for Lester to cave in to his curiosity and call him back to open a more fruitful dialogue.

In the meantime, there were a hundred other things to manage. As he was began sifting through his long-neglected mail, Rupert walked in the office and sat down noisily in the huge couch off to the side, so that Daven was forced to turn around to talk to him.

"Where have you been?"

Rupert made a face. "Conference call with the PR team. You know, the one you are supposed to join every day but keep neglecting, so maybe I should be the one asking where *you've* been?"

"On the phone with Lester Boyd."

"Well, well. So that's the mystery man. Sleeping with the enemy at last, eh?" Rupe grinned.

Daven looked startled. "Absolutely not. How did you come to that conclusion?"

"Never mind, that's not what...forget it. I suppose you told him we know our man was framed, even though I said we shouldn't let that cat out of the bag just yet?"

Daven stood up and looked out the window, gazing to the far reaches of the Pacific Ocean. "I did tell him, and his reaction indicated he was shocked to hear such an accusation. Honestly...now I don't think he's as closely connected to the party as we thought he was. Perhaps my entire theory has been misguided."

"So if he's a nobody, why did he get assigned to babysit Hank's kids, then? That doesn't make any sense, Dav."

"I know. I'll work it out. We have time. Anybody on the team have more guesses as to why Hank rolled over so easily?"

"Said it before, but we still think he was out of his goddamn mind is all."

"I don't think he lost his mind. You know him, he was up to something big. I just wish he had told us what it was before he got himself killed."

Rupert sighed heavily. "Taylor's theory still might hold water: Harmon's minions threatened his kids and forced him into a confession."

"I thought of that, too. But Hank had the option to have me assume guardianship, and he didn't take it. They could've been safe in my home in a heartbeat, but he *willingly* had them taken away and then died for it less than a week later. For nothing. Not only that, but whatever we think about Harmon's party on other issues, their leadership wouldn't abide threatening children. I just don't understand any of this!"

He threw his notebook onto the chair in frustration and went to make another espresso, the third one of the day so far. It wasn't doing anything for him at this point but making him more agitated; he shouldn't have another and ignored his colleague's raised eyebrows that said exactly the same. But Rupe kept his mouth shut; everyone who knew Daven had at some point learned the hard way not to comment on his caffeine addiction.

"Well…at the very least, Hank really threw the Urbanes out of whack. They ousted more aides today, and I've heard more heads are on the chopping block."

Daven nodded. "It does seem strange that we're getting all the good press considering only the two of us know Hank's a martyr and not a traitor. And donations are going through the roof. If I believed in karma, this case would be a prime example for study."

Rupert nodded solemnly. "Absolutely. And what about his sons?"

"I don't know if we can get them back, and I can't afford to focus on them right now. Finding out what Hank was up to has to take precedence." He drank down the espresso in a single gulp and picked up the notebook again, tapping it irregularly as he decisively plotted his next move.

"Rupe…I'm really going to need your help finding out everything there is to know about this Lester Boyd."

Undisclosed location, Virginia

The first week at Bonded Retainer Training School for Minors passed almost without incident. Sure, Theo was highly prone to childish outbursts over small things, but Floyd fought to remember that it occurred precisely because he *was* still a child and understandably upset that life had changed so drastically, virtually overnight.

The humble, diligent, and endlessly dutiful 16-year old Floyd had never been spoiled by Hank Bancroft's power and lifestyle. He didn't care about material things, and was kind to the servants and butler almost to the point of obsequiousness. Their quiet loyalty and devotion to him helped him stay out of trouble. He was well known for sneaking them money and forbidden items, and secretly throwing birthday parties for them in the expansive basements that served as their quarters. Floyd was already keenly missing them after just a few weeks of being apart.

Theo had always been nice to the servants, but aloof. He didn't dare gift them anything after being caught just once. However, he loved the lavish Bancroft lifestyle. Relished it. At twelve, his precocious imagination had already conjured up a veritable timeline of pleasure and indulgence that he was insistent upon being able to experience. But he also wanted to go to college, to be married, to have a different car to drive every day of the week, to have season tickets for a sports team. The list was endless. He wanted his *own* servants.

He hadn't come to terms yet with the fact that none of the goals would ever be achievable now - except perhaps marriage once he was freed. Floyd needed to make him understand, but Theo wasn't ready for that talk yet. He was still asking when they were going to go home, when they were going to see dad again, when he would be able to reunite with his dogs. So far

Floyd had deflected the questions, even knowing he deserved answers...which would most likely never satisfy him.

After all, how do you explain to a 12-year old that the next 20 years of his life belonged to the enemies of your father, and that he had to do well with the opportunity he was given - which wasn't much, admittedly - or else he would suffer even more? Considering the seriousness of the accusations that had taken down Hank Bancroft, they were lucky they had any chance at all for a halfway decent life. And being a house servant wasn't nearly as terrible as some of the other options.

Without that talk, things escalated quickly and Theo went into a crisis on the first day of week two, when half the class was busy preparing lunch for the entire class. First, he refused to do anything except stare at the wall and hum. Floyd talked him out of that, but then, as they were learning how to pluck birds and check the temperature of meats, when Theo threw down the thermometer and yelled, "this is why we have a chef!" At first Floyd thought he was joking, but that was not the case. He bent down to pick up the wand and quickly handed it back to Theo, fearful of what their temperamental kitchen trainer was going to do.

"Quiet, Theo!" he barked in a low tone. "You know we don't have Chef anymore."

"Yes we do, and he's waiting for us. Probably has lunch on the table right now! I want to go home!" And with that, Theo shoved everything off of the kitchen island onto the ground and ran out the door. Blood and juices from uncooked steak and pheasants splattered everywhere, along with broken glass from all goblets that had been waiting to be filled with (fake) wine.

Floyd didn't dare chase him; he couldn't afford another warning. He raised a hand and waited for the trainer to look at him, and then blurted, "May I go and get him-"

"No," said the trainer icily, as he turned to retrieve a box of gloves from a shelf and set it down on the counter. "Clean this mess up, now. All of you. Then you can let everyone know who to thank for missing lunch today."

"But we can still make all the sides," Floyd insisted. "They don't have to go without, please, sir."

He gestured around the room. "We don't have the time. The kitchen and floor needs to be thoroughly sanitized. This is a good lesson, actually. Almost a case study. In real life, you see, Theodore would lose his job immediately and the rest of you would have to clean it up for him anyway. This is-”

“I’ll clean it up myself if you’ll just let them make something for-”

“Have you forgotten this morning’s penalty for speaking out of turn? If so, I'm happy to repeat it for clarification."

Everyone now turned to gape at Floyd in shocked silence, so he flushed, took the gloves, and bent down to start cleaning, first taking a moment to study his aching palms that were criss-crossed with raised welts. Sliding the blue gloves on was agony. His throat suddenly swelled with grief; Dad was a strict disciplinarian, too, but he would never dream of doing such a cruel thing to his boys. Floyd missed him terribly and was counting down the days until it was time for yearly visitation. Only 350 days left...

While working on mopping up the rest of the blood from Theo’s tirade, Floyd calmed himself and resolutely decided to stop delaying and have *the talk* with his little brother. But first, he needed to talk to their guidance counselor and see if he could offer some advice.

CHAPTER TWO

MAYFAIR FEDERAL PRISON, PENNSYLVANIA

"Jesus Christ, Hank," muttered Lester as he plopped down on the other side of the visitor's booth, slapping down a thick file folder onto the counter. "What a bloody mess you've gotten yourself into."

"Lester?" Hank queried in disbelief as he squinted his eyes, reached forward, and hooked his fingers into the wire partition that was separating them. "Is that....is that you?"

"In the flesh. Been a long time."

"Holy shit. What...how... *what the fuck are you doing here?*"

"I got asked to be here. Calm down, let's talk like gentlemen. It's just you and me, and we have a lot to cover."

Hank was so taken aback that he literally could not get the mechanisms in his throat to work in order to enable to him to respond - had he anything to say, that is. For now, all he could do was stare and gape. So Lester dived right in.

"Harmon has appointed me as the negotiator for this discussion, prior to the arraignment tomorrow. You do know that's happening tomorrow, right? I don't know what they've told you."

Hank continued to stare, and Lester gave it right back to him. Several long moments passed.

"What. *the fuck.* are you doing. *here*," Hank repeated, having almost recovered from the shock. There was no anger in the question, although there should be, considering what happened the last time they saw each other.

"As I said," Lester repeated calmly, although he felt like passing out from anxiety, "I'm a pre-arraignment negotiator. Appointed by Harmon himself."

Hank stood up and walked away, pacing his little booth fruitlessly, hoping to exit. There was no guard to let him out, though, and after pounding on the door a few times without response, he stood against the back wall as far as he could go, glaring daggers at his former friend.

"Yes, I know the arraignment is tomorrow, to answer your question. But this makes absolutely zero sense. I repeat: *why are you here?* I heard you were a teacher and that you left the Urbanes. Turns out you're still Harmon's little bitch, huh?"

"Never was his bitch. If anything, he was mine. I'm actually here to talk about Theo and Floyd…more specifically, to discuss their future when you're found guilty. Harmon chose me for obvious reasons, but if you need me to spell them out, I will."

Hank said nothing. Harmon of course knew that Lester had loved the boys once, so…yes, this made sense now. But that didn't mean it was acceptable.

"Are you going to talk to me, or just stare at me like I have three heads?" Lester asked harshly. "Sit down, Hank. We have one hour."

Hank growled, "So Harmon has some fucking balls, after all. Who knew. Sending you, of all people, to threaten my sons in the same breath you claim to still love them. I'm perfectly happy to just stand here and stare at you for 54 more minutes.”

“You see me threatening anyone? I’m here to help them.”

Hank snorted. “Right. Help. What do you want, exactly?”

“To be precise, I want you to sit down in front of me and talk about old times for a minute or so. Then we’ll talk about the future. There will be no more arguing from my end, but you’re welcome to it if it makes you feel better. Just don’t expect me to reciprocate. Now sit the hell down.”

Lester watched as Hank gauged his expression critically, then crossed the room and sat down heavily. He smiled sardonically and pitched his tone up to an excessively cheerful tenor.

“So, Lester, old friend. How have you been? Life treating you well? Divorced yet? Got kids? Been on vacation? Do tell.”

Lester sighed. “Fine. Not really. Widower. No kids, she miscarried twice. Forgot what the word vacation even means. Anything else?”

"Not for the moment," Hank replied in a much gentler tone, feeling like total shit suddenly as the lump in his throat doubled. "I'm very sorry to hear about Karen. What happened?"

Lester ignored that. "Listen up, Hank. These charges...if you plead not guilty against the evidence, the trial is going to be an absolute shit show. Even without it, you must know the jury will be heavily prejudiced against you, especially with your recent tirade against your own constituents."

"It wasn't a tirade, it was a...forget that! I thought you were only here to discuss the boys," Hank replied sharply, pounding the counter as he did so.

"In a minute." He picked up the file. "Bribery of state officials. Abuse of the public trust. Corporate espionage...that's the one that allowed Harmon in the game when he decided to bring criminal charges. Blackmail. I'm not here to discuss your guilt or innocence, but-"

"I won't be found guilty of anything," Hank responded confidently. "These charges were only brought three days ago, but-"

"Yes, you will. That's why I'm here."

Now Hank looked at him like he really *did* have three heads. "What are you saying?"

Lester took a deep breath and lowered his voice. "I'm saying…look, it's really difficult to say this to you, but I have to. Hank, this is so bad that *your own party* decided to lock you up, not us. This is their doing. I'm not the enemy. Harmon's not the enemy, at least not right now. I'm just wondering how the hell it was *you* that finally brought down the Seditionists? I mean, perhaps I should be saying thank you, but damn, I'm just as confused as everyone else. This is unprecedented. It's sensational."

"My own party turned me in, huh? Jesus, you got to stop listening to Hailey. If you're already convinced of my guilt, why are you here?"

"As I said, to help-"

Hank interrupted furiously, "If Harmon really thinks I'm done for, he should be doing handstands and throwing a party right about now, not sending in a negotiator. I would appreciate if you would get to the point."

Lester's eyes narrowed. "What part of *I'm here to help your sons* are you not getting?"

Hank grinned. "I can still read you like a book after all these years, Lester. You're threatening them because a trial could prompt me to expose things my double agents found that would bring down Harmon, should I decide to bargain with the government instead of you. This is such an obvious ploy that I'm almost disappointed at the lack of suspense."

Lester hesitated for the first time, and felt unsure of his own footing for a few moments. Hank wasn't wrong about the party's motives where Harmon was concerned, but no one was threatening the boys. Lester would never have agreed to such a tactic, and neither would Harmon - who, ironically, was the one with the more humane constituents and party policies.

"Alright, Hank. Let's put emotions aside and talk facts instead for the moment. If you are found guilty by trial on or after April 1, your boys will be deeded to the state for life. And that's whether you spend 48 hours or 48 years in jail. It's automatic, no negotiation. You know that already, I assume?"

Hank nodded wordlessly. He was pale and sweaty all of a sudden.

Lester softened his tone, hating himself for what he had to say next. "The Urbanes can propose a plea deal in which that does not occur, but you must plead guilty and agree to immediate execution. Before you decide, I'll remind you one last time that your conviction on at least one count is certain."

Lester reached over to the tape recorder and hit play. Hank listened to himself blackmailing Harmon, then sat stone-faced and said nothing, even long after the recording ended. He'd had no idea that tape existed until a few days ago. Those remarks to his chief rival had been sarcastic, joking even, made in a moment of anger...but no jury in their right mind could say it was anything but outright blackmail. *Fuck.*

Lester cleared his throat harshly. "Hank, the deal is simple. You plead no contest, agree to execution, and the boys will be taken care of."

"I am *not* negotiating," Hank fired back. "The answer is no. Go fuck yourself."

Lester shrugged and stood up as if to leave. "Fine. Then you have zero chance of wrapping this up before April 1, and the deeds to the boys will go to the state. If you're fine with that, I'll just take my leave now."

Hank's expression could have set the world on fire in its intensity. He leaned forward, thankful for the wire barricade that would stop him from adding homicide to the long list of charges against him.

"You son of a bitch," he growled dangerously. "Don't you walk away from me again."

Seditionists HQ, Los Angeles

It was 9pm, and Daven hadn't even sifted through half of his much-despised email for the day yet. It seemed like for every one he answered, two more would appear in his box to take its place. How was this technology supposed to make life easier?

he wondered for the hundredth time. All it did was create more work in a shorter time span.

The desk phone rang. Dav leaned over to press the speakerphone button and dumped half a cup of espresso into his lap at the same time.

"Fuck," he blurted as he leaped up to snatch a handful of napkins from the sideboard.

"Not right now, honey, I have a headache," Hank retorted with a snort.

"Oh. Sorry to hear that. I have ibuprofen and Aleve."

Hank rolled his eyes and sighed. "Hey, call it a night already, would you? Your office light is keeping me awake down here."

Daven leaned all the way over his desk and looked out the door down the hallway. Hank was doing the same from his office, but the lights were off.

"You're sleeping in the office? Did something happen at the house?"

There was a bark of laughter from the dark office. "No, I'm actually heading out. Floyd isn't feeling well. Hang up, I'm coming over."

Hank gathered up his coat and briefcase and strolled into Daven's office.

"Look, I know you don't celebrate Christmas and all, but I wish you'd reconsider for once. You've never come once in 6 years. It's going to be a hell of a party."

Daven dabbed feverishly at his slacks with a comically large stack of cocktail napkins. "I'm not sure I would enjoy a party described as *hellish*, Hank. Please forgive me for passing it up."

Bancroft Manor, Christmas Eve

Daven went to the party, of course. He wasn't nearly as immune to his boss's charms as he wished he could be; the man could get literally anyone to do anything he wanted. After giving his coat to a house servant and heading to the bar for a glass of water, his phone rang noisily.

Unknown number.

Daven never answered unknown numbers, and he proceeded to ignore it the next five times it rang with a call as well. On the seventh time, however, his curiosity got the best of him and he pulled it back out of his pocket and decided to answer. Since his voice as the speaker of the party was so well-known and constantly mimicked, he pitched it up a bit to avoid the caller identifying the number as his.

"Yes?" he answered. "Who is calling?"

"Do you have a moment to speak in private, Daven? It's important."

Daven moved outside to a quiet corner of the patio, interest now greatly piqued. "I think you have the wrong number," he tried hopefully. "But if you tell me what it's about, maybe I can point you in the right direction."

"I am calling on the emergency line with some information that you personally need to hear. Immediately. And I know this is Daven, so please don't keep pretending I have the wrong number."

Daven's blood went cold. That's why the caller got directed to this phone; the emergency number that was given to all undercover agents was diverted to an unlisted office line, which was currently forwarded to his cell. He had never actually received one of these calls before.

"I'm listening. Please proceed."

"Only if you promise to look in this immediately. I'm risking everything to call you right now. But I trust you with my life to do what you'll say you'll do."

"I promise I will address it immediately. Tell me what's going on."

"Political treason, Daven, plain and simple. Four days ago Hank Bancroft paid a leader of the Urbanes to plant an agent within the government, who would be working on behalf of the Urbanes. I was there, because I happened to be the particular agent that was chosen for the task. The problem is, I already work for you guys. For us, rather. So I'm bugging out, and I'll need you to send me relocation and restart compensation. *Without* getting Hank involved, obviously."

Holy shit. There were almost 50 agents working undercover in Urbane territory, and it was absolutely certain this man's cover would be blown fairly quickly, if not the very instant he set foot in the capital. That's why his career was over, and the party would have to pay for it no matter what happened next.

Daven cleared his throat and tried to sound unconcerned. "Look, I know you have a verification code that can prove your identity, but I'm not in my office and can't cross-check it. You have to call me back tomorrow at 8am Pacific, okay? Don't say anything else until then."

"Will do. I can explain further, but got to run now. They're making my arrangements to leave for the Capital and I'll go, but somehow on the way there-"

"I can't say anything more until you're verified. I have to end this call now. You must call me tomorrow at 8am and no later. Be careful."

He disconnected the call and carefully set his face expressionless as Hank approached him and offered a glass of champagne, which Daven reluctantly took.

"Merry Christmas, Dav. You're standing under the mistletoe, so that means I get to kiss you now. Always wanted to do that, actually," he joked easily. A little alcohol always loosened him up enough to flirt with just about anybody.

"Maybe later, Hank. We need to talk. Can we go somewhere private?"

"Ooh, moving so fast. I hope we'll be doing more than talking," Hank teased again, although there was absolutely nothing meant by it other than to make his subordinate blush.

"I'm serious, boss. I just received an emergency call that you need to know about immediately."

That sorted Hank out; he led the way to his first floor library, far from the opposite wing of the house where the party was taking place.

Hank was no longer interested in his wine and set it down on the sideboard as he closed the door.

"What's up, Dav? You've got my adrenaline going, so let's hear it."

"The Urbanes are about to make one of our agents. I don't know who he is yet, but he's going to call me back."

"Well, shit. Get Taylor to start the relocation process, then. That's unfortunate. What exactly did he say?"

Daven took a deep breath and tried not to let his nervousness show.

"He said...well, it was about a meeting you had on Tuesday. He is deeply concerned that you were misled about the man's identity and motives. Seems the outcome of that meeting was this agent being chosen for a mission for the Urbanes which he cannot undertake or decline without being exposed."

It wasn't the whole truth… but it wasn't a lie, either.

"Jesus," Hank breathed heavily. "I had five or six meetings that day. Did he say which one?"

"No." *Here goes nothing*, Daven thought. "But if you get me a list of who you met with, I'll look into them immediately. We should be able to pin it down quickly."

Hank looked a little startled. "Did you verify this agent's identity?"

"Uh, no. Not yet."

Hank looked annoyed. "Oh come on Dav, you know better than to talk to unverified callers on that line! Do that first, and then I'll get you the list. For all we know, he was captured and is calling under duress. The code he gives will tell us."

"But we should get started right away-"

"No. There's also the possibility he got cold feet and wants to disappear on our dime. When's he going to call back?"

Daven had never lied to Hank before - even when he probably should have - and wasn't about to start now. "Tomorrow at 8am."

"Christmas day? Nice."

"Hank, don't you think it's best if we start to check up on those names right now? Why wait?"

"Dav, I *think* we should enjoy this party. It's Christmas eve. Come on."

Hank swept his wine off the sideboard and disappeared without another glance at his colleague and friend. Daven watched him go, his heart suddenly heavy with uncertainty. If Hank insisted on joining him to hear the agent's call, things were about to get *very* complicated.

Merry Christmas, indeed..

CHAPTER THREE

Bonded Retainer Training School for Minors - Virginia

Lester Boyd made his way to his office and glanced at the day's agenda that his secretary prepared for him every morning. He was incredulous upon seeing Floyd and Theo Bancroft's names on his visitor list for the day, for the third time in ten days. The boys could not stay out of trouble if their lives depended on it. If he didn't get them under control fast, everything he had done to keep them safe would be ultimately pointless. It was time to lay down the law.

"Theo was freaking out in kitchen class, sir, and he....I just went after him about it and we-"

"What do you mean, *went after him* ?"

Floyd swallowed his resentment at the whole affair and kept his tone level. "I don't think he's taking our situation seriously enough. I got mad and yelled at him in front of everyone, and then I hit him. I don't regret it and would do the same thing all over again to keep him safe. He has no idea what's going to happen to us if we don't finish this training, because I keep....I just...I need your help. Please."

Lester groaned inwardly; had he known this, he wouldn't have been so harsh in his lecture. It was clear there was a lot more going on than he bargained for with the young Bancrofts.

"I see. Floyd, you're out of verbal warnings already. The next one's written. Seven written warnings means you're deeded to the state, and no one besides me is going to care what your excuse is. I've been force to eject students in week 25, and that could happen to you if you don't keep yourself under control, immediately. You have a long way to go and need to choose your battles wisely. Do we understand each other?"

Floyd looked absolutely crushed. What battles could be more important than those he fought to protect Theo? "Yes, sir, but-"

"No buts. We're still in week two. I had high hopes for you, but to be honest, right now I'm really disappointed at your lack of common sense and control. I have 60 students to handle and just the two of you have taken up all of my time since you arrived. Your brother is waiting outside. Call him in to stand with you, and you're not to say a single word until I address you directly. I mean it."

Floyd froze, his increasing panic not allowing for any verbal response.

"Go get your brother," Mr. Boyd repeated, a little more gently this time.

Floyd propelled himself out the door and spotted Theo standing dejectedly by the water fountain on the other side of the hall and called him over. To his credit, Theo hurried to his side without hesitation and looked sufficiently abashed.

"I'm so sorry, Floyd. Are you okay?"

"For now. But if you mouth off again, I swear to-"

"I won't!"

"Then get in there, and behave yourself." Floyd gave vent to his frustration by shoving Theo through the doorway as they passed through, a movement that caused Lester to raise his eyebrows in dismay. Floyd looked at the floor, feeling ashamed of himself.

"Floyd," Lester said in a warning tone, but then turned to Theo without further comment. "Theodore. I'm going to repeat what I just told your brother. Seven written warnings of any kind and you're automatically deeded to the state. Period. Do you understand what that means?"

"I'm sure I'll find out soon enough," was the mumbled reply.

"I'm going to pretend you didn't say that. Now, not only did you damage property and ruin the food, I also have a report here of you fooling around the day before and carving 'anatomical pictures' into fruit with a melon baller. Shockingly enough, you're not the first genius to have thought of that. Just wait to see what happens when you all advance to cucumber canapés."

Floyd glanced at Theo, fearing he would start laughing all over again.

Theo was not in the mood for comedy, however. He wanted to argue. "That was harmless. I can't believe I got in trouble for that."

"Anything you get in trouble for is designed to protect you. When you're placed as a house servant, behavior like that will cost you your job. And that, in turn, will mean you're automatically reduced to the lowest tier of service for the state. For life. No second chances. Do you even know what the lowest tier is, Theodore?"

Floyd answered quickly, "Manual labor."

Lester sighed and reached into his desk. "You're speaking out of turn, Floyd. Lucky for you, I don't give warnings for that. Hold out your hands."

Floyd complied, eyes wide, while Lester stepped around the desk and quickly laid down one stripe across each palm with a thin cane. It was shockingly painful over the existing welts, and Floyd hissed and immediately began rubbing his hands together while tears sprouted unchecked from both eyes. Mr. Boyd considered this "lucky?"

Theo was staring agape at them, turning white as a sheet. Neither of them had any experience with this particular form of discipline, as Hank Bancroft openly considered corporal punishment on anything other than spanking the backside of children to be barbaric. It was part of the reason he had been so openly in conflict with his own constituents, who wished to bring back public floggings and were very close to succeeding in getting a measure drawn in the House.

Lester replaced the implement in his drawer and Floyd could see he clearly regretted having to take the action, but it was better than using up another warning. Floyd reminded himself to thank him later...maybe it was lucky, after all, but it sure didn't feel like it right now.

"Now, let's try this again. Theodore, do you know what the lowest tier is that you can be assigned to?"

"You just hit my brother!" Theo blurted out hotly. Floyd almost told him to shut up, but held back at the last millisecond and swallowed down his emotion. He wasn't resentful, or even remotely angry, about what had happened. He was just scared out of his wits for his brother.

"Theo, *answer him* ," Floyd whispered.

Theo looked like he was about to answer, but then he set his shoulders in *that* way that had always made Floyd and his father want to scream.

"Can you repeat the question?" he replied with a smirk.

"Do you know what the lowest tier of indentured servitude is that you can be assigned to?"

"Yes. And I also know you've now ended a question twice with a preposition."

"Yes, I did. But you started a sentence with 'and.' I'm not sure what is worse."

"*Which* is worse."

"That should be phrased as a question," retorted Lester lightly.

"Whatever. This is stupid," complained Theo bitterly.

It was taking everything Floyd had not to leap over and throttle his brother. He had kept himself occupied during this bizarre debate by wringing his palms together to help stave off the increasing pain, but it wasn't working.

"Stop being a fucking idiot, Theo!" Floyd turned and growled, being completely unable to hold his tongue any longer.

"Floyd, be still," Lester said sharply as he glanced over at him, although there was a definite glint of amusement in his expression. "Your brother and I were just discussing proper grammar techniques, everything's fine."

"Yeah. Shut up, Floyd, unless you can contribute something to the conversation."

Floyd and Theo immediately erupted into the petty bickering that young teenage boys do. So much for employing humor as a disarming tactic. Far from that, it had backfired spectacularly; Floyd was visibly ready to tackle the brat and beat him senseless, and there wasn't much holding him back any longer.

"Boys!"

They stopped their arguing abruptly and looked down at the floor.

"You're obviously intelligent enough to grasp what you're doing wrong, so I won't spell it out. I just have one question: can you get your shit together before I'm forced to replace you with new students from the waiting list? I assure you, at this rate I'll be making that decision in less than a week."

"Let them in. It's a stupid program anyway," Theo responded petulantly. "Melon balls? I mean, come on."

"I'm so sorry," blurted Floyd desperately, in tears again. House servitude was the only program that guaranteed them both placement together in the same workplace if they successfully passed it. They were lucky to be here, and he was furious at Theo for not seeing that. "Can we just...can I call my dad and have him talk to Theody? He will set him straight, I promise. Please don't kick us out."

Lester's heart dropped, and he had to take in a long, deep breath to steady himself.

"You know you can't call him," he responded gently. "Neither can I. Theodore, I'm not your enemy. Do you understand that?"

"Right," he huffed, almost to himself. "That's why you can just beat us on the spot whenever you feel like it. Go ahead, seize the *opportunity*."

Emphasis on the last word, just to throw it in his face that they were not cut from the same cloth.

Theo held his palms out and glanced at Floyd, expecting and perhaps looking forward to another round of swearing, but he was ignoring them and absently picking at the buttons on his coat. Already defeated. Depressed. Lost.

Lester saw it, too. "Put your hands down. I understand your situation is unusually tough, and I'm willing to let your attitude slide until you adjust. But you must answer a question before you can go. I want to remind you that your indenture as a house servant is for 20 years. If you fail with this behavior, which is imminent...meaning, you're on the path to fail in just a few days...you will be deeded to the state *for life*. You have no other options, period. So I have to ask: are you going to try and get through this program, or not?"

"Yes, sir. I'm sorry," Theo replied quietly, without any trace of rancor. Floyd was pleasantly surprised at how quickly he became compliant - especially after being threatened, which was usually the fastest route to a massive temper tantrum. He did not realize that was Theo had seen Floyd's grief and was really apologizing to him, not their mentor.

"Floyd? How about you?"

"Yes, sir. Please forgive us, we've...it's been..."

"Forgiven. One last thing. It was a mistake to have you room together. I'm going to split you up-"

"No, wait-" sputtered Floyd.

"I don't want to hear it. Theo, dismissed. Go pack your bag and get ready to move."

Theo left wearily, wisely refraining from spouting off again as he went, and Floyd did all he could not to dissolve again in front of his counselor.

"Floyd, don't start that puppy dog eyes crap with me. A blind fool could see that you're spending too much time together and all he's doing is entertaining himself by pushing every button you have. I'm going to put him in a room by himself and that's the end of it. If and when I'm ready to reconsider, I will let you know. Clear?"

"I don't understand why you're doing this," Floyd muttered. "Please tell me why."

"Why I'm being so nice to you, you mean?" Lester responded calmly. "You asked me to help your brother, and this is part of how I'm going to do it. He needs his space for the time being. You can visit him during the free hour each evening. There's nothing more I want than to see the two of you *not* thrown into state custody. For now, you're the one causing the most trouble, not him. So keep it together and behave yourself."

Floyd immediately got the point, took a deep breath, and looked him straight in the eyes. "Thank you for what you're trying to do, Mr. Boyd. I'm sorry my brother doesn't appreciate it, but I do."

"No one ever does. You're a rare one. One last thing: Theo's discipline is not your job, it's mine. If you ever manhandle him again on my watch, you won't be able to sit down for a week. Clear? Good. Dismissed."

He watched Floyd trudge out, hating that he had to be so harsh with him. He still wasn't sure whether to be grateful or hurt that neither of the boys yet recognized their "Uncle" Lester from so long ago. It certainly did make things less complicated, but Floyd's plea for Lester to call his father to help Theo nearly broke his heart in a hundred pieces.

The boys did not know Hank was already dead, and Lester was under strict orders not to tell them until Harmon gave him permission to do so.

Christmas Day

Seditionists HQ, Los Angeles

Daven arrived at the office at 7am, eager to hear back from the agent regarding the intel he had passed along during Hank's Christmas party. First things first - he had to identify the agent. There were five individualized codes that the man had to memorize upon his first day of work, and each of them had a separate purpose to be used to calls to their superiors or the emergency line:

1 - agent reporting normally

2 - agent reporting under duress, information is accurate

3 - agent reporting under duress, information is false

4 - agent is made, attempt a rescue

5 - agent is made, do not attempt rescue

Depending on what code the man gave, Dav would know the situation immediately and be able to act accordingly. His predecessor had been the one to take these calls; this was his first, and the anxiety was almost unbearable for several reasons.

Obviously, the first reason was because of the reason for the call. Number 3 in this case would be the best scenario in regards to what he had said about Hank. Number 1 would be the worst case.

Then, there was the problem about him having honestly told Hank the time that the agent was going to be calling. He wished he had lied. As a preventative measure, he had pulled Rupert aside at the Christmas party and asked him to help get Hank as drunk as possible. The man's hangovers were few but epic, and if anything could prevent him from showing up at the office at 8am, that would be the thing to do it. Rupert hadn't asked questions, and Daven watched him bring glass after glass to their boss.

The last thing causing him such anxiety was the idea that he might have to go behind Hank's back to get the full story, and that was the worst part. In ten years they had worked together, neither of them had expressed any desire to be dishonest towards each other for any reason, for better or worse. And sometimes it was for the worst, but it never caused any longstanding friction between them.

Daven had never lied, not once, and he believed it was the same with Hank. At least, he hoped it was so.

At 7:50am Daven laid the book of identifying codes out in front of him, then stood at the window to watch the parking lot while he was on the phone. If Hank did show up, at least he would get advanced notice and could perhaps warn the agent.

A moment later his phone rang, startling him enough that he jumped away from the window and nearly fell over the horrible fluffy chair that he had been unsuccessfully trying to get removed from his office for as long as he could remember.

"Good morning, Hank," Daven answered, trying to sound completely normal.

"Ugh. Don't talk so loud."

"Sorry."

"Just got to the office, but I forgot my badge. Can you come downstairs and swipe me in? I'm at the backdoor."

Shit. Shit. Shit.

"Sure. Be right there. Should I get an espresso going for you, too?"

"Yeah. Thanks."

Daven hung up the phone and pressed the button to pre-heat the water, then made his way to the elevator with a pounding heart.

He should have lied. *God damn it.*

As they entered his office and Hank draped himself across Rupe's chair, flinging an arm over his face to shield his eyes from the sun, Daven prepared the espresso for his boss without speaking. He didn't know what to say, in any case, there was no time. It was almost 8am.

He handed the cup to Hank, who blew on it for some time before asking, "You think he's going to call? Hope he's alright."

"I hope so."

"Hmm. Sorry to ask, but do you mind closing the blinds?"

Daven nodded and closed them wordlessly.

"Thanks. You okay, Dav? You seem nervous."

Nervous. If you only knew.

"I am. Listen, Hank, he...he wants to talk to me alone. I'm not sure he will agree to say a word if you're listening. Apparently he knows me and trusts me, but it doesn't appear he knows you."

"Or trusts me, maybe. That's fine. Don't tell him I'm on the line, then."

"But what if-"

"This isn't negotiable. Dav, please don't ask me such a thing ever again. I'm the goddamned leader of the party, in case you forgot."

Daven clamped his mouth shut. Hank rarely pulled rank, but when he did, he meant business.

"And while I'm at it," Hank continued sternly as he peered at Dav through half-closed eyelids, "I will nail your ass to the wall if you ever converse with an unverified asset again, do you hear me?"

"You are right on both counts, of course. My deepest apologies."

Hank leaned back and threw his arm over his eyes again, and fell silent. It was an expected and well-deserved chastisement, and Daven was relieved to get off so easy.

But he still couldn't shake the deep feeling of dread that had darkened his thoughts since first hearing the agent's intel. At 7:59 Daven lifted his cell phone, made sure Hank wasn't looking, and discreetly toggled the satellite connection to OFF.

Then he sat down to wait for the call that could never come.

CHAPTER FOUR

BRTSM, Virginia

"I need your help again, Olivia," Lester said gently into the phone. "I got to start finding a place for two brothers for five months. A good one, no history of abuse or a bunch of turnover in the household. If you have any ideas, please let me know. They'll be ready to enter service on December first. Can you ask around and see who's looking for new servants? You have my number, call me back when you can. Thanks a ton."

He hung up and turned to the next phone number of his list of closest friends within the party. "Hey Hailey, it's Lester Boyd. Listen... I need your help with some more of my boys. I've got two good ones, 12 and 16, who need to be placed together. I know you're connected to the Hannigans, so can you poke around with them and see if they need anyone in one of their estates, or if they know anyone who does? Call me back as soon as you can, thanks so much."

There was one more number in his contacts with no name attached. As usual, he stared at it thoughtfully for a while and debated calling it just to see who would answer, but set it aside for the hundredth time. The boys were due any minute now for their weekly review, and he was as nervous as a wet cat. Floyd had been giving him strange looks lately, and it was possible he had figured out who Lester was, or maybe not. Not that it would mean anything had to change if he did, but it would make it a lot harder to keep threatening to kick them out; the fact that they just might put two and two together and call his bluff was always in the back of his mind.

The phone rang a minute later at the exact same time as they knock on the door. Lester yelled "come in!" at the same time he lifted the receiver, fully expecting it to be one of the school administrators to remind him of some faculty meeting or another. His phone didn't have caller ID, though, so pretty much every call was a surprise.

"Hello."

There was a long pause.

"Hello?" he repeated.

"Who is this, please?" said the gruff voice on the other line. "Just want to make sure I have the right number."

Theo and Floyd shuffled in, eyes darting about warily. Lester held a hand up to stop them from saying anything, and focused on the caller.

"Nice try. Who are *you* ?"

Another long pause. "I see we are at an impasse. Very well. I received your number from Hank Bancroft some time ago, but I was not in a position to call until now. Can you talk? It's important."

Holy smokes. *What the hell...*

"I'm in a meeting. Let me take your number and call you back."

"Not possible. When is a good time to call you back?"

Lester looked at Theo and Floyd, who seemed just as intensely curious about the caller as he was. Then a light bulb went off and he grabbed the notebook he had recently set aside, and looked at the last number without really needing to. It was all but seared into his brain.

"Okay, let me read that back to you," Lester said slyly. It was a big gamble, but there was no other reasonable explanation. "310-758-5100. Is that right?"

A brief pause, now. "No. I'm not sure who's number that is. When would be a good time to call you back?" the voice repeated, a little more tension evident than before.

"Actually, I'm not interested. Please remove my number from your database. Have a good day."

He hung up the phone with numb hands and tried to remember to breathe normally. This kind of subterfuge was a thing of the past, better left there, and an unshakable feeling of ill-omen gripped him hard. He couldn't think for a few moments, and cursed Hank silently for putting him in the middle of god knows what.

"Damned telemarketing calls," he muttered as he reached behind the phone to unplug the cord, then changed the subject as quickly as he could get away with. "Theodore, I heard you made another ruckus in kitchen class yesterday. I'm supposed to give you grief about it, so what happened?"

"If I wanted to be a chef, I could have gone to cooking school. This is stupid!"

"We're not training you to be a chef!" Lester blurted impatiently. "You're a house servant, and nothing more. If you don't behave yourself, you won't even be that. If you haven't grasped that concept yet since our last conversation, maybe I should just kick you out now and save all of us the time and grief."

Theo and Floyd both looked absolutely crushed by this outburst, and Lester realized he had completely lost his grip on his temper and unfairly taken it out on the boys. The mysterious call had rattled him a lot more than he would be willing to admit. He calmed himself down, but decided not to apologize. Theo was acting stupidly and it wouldn't hurt to call him out on it.

"Speaking of which, I fully expect that you both did the research I asked you for on exactly what it means to be deeded to the state. What did you learn, Theo?"

"I..." he was still shocked from Lester's outburst and couldn't respond.

"I'll get back to you. Floyd? Same question."

"I learned that I would rather die, sir." He had unshed tears in his eyes; perhaps from Lester's outburst, but most likely caused by the fact he had discovered that siblings were always separated into different facilities and were extremely unlikely to find each other again.

"Good takeaway. Discouragement was the point of the exercise, after all. Theo, back to you."

"Same answer, sir," he managed to choke out.

Lester had almost forgotten about the mysterious caller at this point, since both boys were now fighting back tears and looked as guilty as beagles caught raiding a trash can. But now the man's voice came back with frightening clarity, and suddenly he couldn't focus on anything else.

"Then we'll consider this review over and lesson learned. Onward and upwards. Dismissed."

They practically ran out, and Lester plugged the phone back in and before the door had even closed he began dialing the number Hank gave him. He needed to know who this man was. But then he stopped himself abruptly and slammed down the phone. The call logs were closely monitored, and he would have an awful lot of explaining to do if someone noticed him calling Los Angeles from his work office. Not if... *when* they noticed.

The number was for a close friend of Hank's family, presumably. Lester had memorized it ever since Hank dictated it to him in their final moments together and made him promise to let the boys call it when they were ready to hear of his death. Lester told Harmon about the exchange, and the party leader agreed to honor the request, but only when he personally gave the go-ahead. That caveat irked Lester to no end, but they weren't ready yet anyway.

At any rate, the strange call had to be reported, even if he couldn't confirm where it came from. He sighed, went to lock the door, said a short prayer, and reluctantly dialed up Colbert.

Floyd was perfectly silent as they made their way back to quarters, but Theo was bursting with excitement.

"Shut up, Theo. Don't say a word. I mean it."

"I can't help it. You heard the number, too, didn't you? Uncle Dav knows where we are! He's going to get us out of here and back to-"

Floyd turned around and pushed him up against the wall, pinning him there in a tight hold.

"Shut. UP. I swear to god I will rip out your throat myself if you ever mention him to me again."

Theo pushed Floyd off of him and wriggled away. "What the fuck are you doing, Floyd?" he whined. "Are you nuts? Aren't you happy he wants to help us?"

Floyd grabbed him roughly and pinned him again, harder this time. "No! Daven is the one who turned in dad!"

"What?!" Theo gasped.

"So you're going to forget about him, and Rupert. Forget that they exist. And besides, the whole world probably knows where we are by now. That call meant nothing, understand? This doesn't change a damned thing. You and I need to fend for ourselves now, and lay low and get through this fucking training before we get separated. You're all I have, and if you-"

"Okay, okay. Stop it, Floyd! I didn't know. Get off me, please." He had stopped fighting, and his face was ashen.

Floyd choked back a sob. "I'm sorry I didn't tell you before. But now...well, now you know. So don't get your hopes up."

He let go, and then pulled his little brother into a tight hug as they both dissolved into long-overdue tears of grief and loss.

"I'm so sorry. Forgive me, Theody..."

Seditionist HQ, Los Angeles

Christmas Day, 1994

8am.

8:30am.

9am.

9:30am.

The phone never rang, of course, and Daven had not said a single word the entire time except to offer Hank another cup of espresso.

10am.

"I don't think he's going to call, Dav," Hank said sleepily. "We should give it another hour, though."

"As you wish," Daven replied curtly, without taking his eyes off of the code book. To say he was on edge was a massive understatement. Every minute that passed by felt like a lifetime in itself.

10:30am.

Daven suddenly bolted noisily upright and dived a hand into his desk drawer, which startled the dozing Hank into complete wakefulness, and not a little bit of confusion.

"What the hell, Dav-"

"Shh! Someone's in the building."

They listened for a good 30 seconds and heard nothing, but then the unmistakable sound of steady footsteps on the metal stairway confirmed Dav's worst fears.

They looked at each other askance; the safe room was in Hank's office and there was no possible way to dart across the long hallway and get into without being seen - or possibly intercepted - by their unauthorized visitor.

Daven cocked the gun that he always kept within arm's reach in a hidden drawer. "Hank, lock yourself in my restroom," he ordered in a whisper.

"What? No!"

The footsteps came closer, and there was the sound of something falling over or being dropped.

"Hank! Get in there!"

"Dad?" came a high-pitched tentative voice from the hallway.

"Floyd?" they both cried out, and a few seconds later the boy appeared around the corner, then gasped and dived back again when he saw Daven's gun.

Hank collected himself quickly and then barked, "Floyd! Get your ass in here." Then, to Dav as he was calmly uncocking his gun and putting it away, "Thank you for not shooting my son, considering I would very much enjoy the satisfaction of doing it myself."

Floyd trudged in, holding Hank's badge that he had forgotten at home. "You're not picking up your phone, so I got in with this."

Hank strode over to him and snatched the badge out of his hand, drawing on every ounce of willpower he had left to stop himself from spinning the boy around and giving him the belting of a lifetime. He would never dream of doing it here in front of Dav, but at home? Different story.

"What *exactly* are you doing here, and how did you get here?" he asked with that kind of dangerous tone that invariably sent Hank's employees, friends, and even family instantly scurrying for cover. But never Floyd; he was either braver or more reckless than most.

"I drove. Dad, Theo hasn't stopped crying for hours. I couldn't stand it anymore. Can you come home?"

Hank was stunned. "*Drove*? Are you serious? Nobody's dying or anything, right? Just checking, because there could be no other acceptable reason for you to-"

"It's Christmas day!" Floyd protested, and water droplets started to form in his eyes. "You said you would never miss another one." And then, absurdly, he looked to Dav and smiled as if nothing was wrong. "Hi Uncle Dav. Merry Christmas."

Daven walked over and embraced Floyd in the warm, crushing kind of bear hug that the boys loved. "Merry Christmas, Floyd. Hey, can you go wait in your dad's office while I talk to him for a minute? It's the one way down at the end of the hall with the green door. Don't stand outside with your ear to this door, okay? Promise me."

Floyd looked to Hank for permission (he knew his father too well to do otherwise), and reluctantly got it. He went out with a sniff, closing the door softly behind him.

Hank glared. "Don't even start on me, Dav. He's my kid and I don't want your opinion on this."

"Actually, what I was going to tell you is that we should wait until 11 for the call, as you said. I'll keep Floyd occupied with my putting green until then. It's only 25 more minutes."

"No, he's going to sit in my office and keep his mouth shut. And tomorrow I'm going to teach him a-"

Daven's office phone rang suddenly, quite loud in the abnormal quiet of the empty office building. They both jumped. Again.

"Sorry," he said, turning around to the phone. "Who on earth is calling me *here,* on a Saturday?"

Hank shrugged. "And on Christmas? No idea."

Daven picked up the receiver. "Yes?"

"Jesus, Dav. Answer your damned cell phone once in a while, will you?"

It was Rupert. Daven's eyes flashed to his phone; the satellite connection was still turned off.

"Rupe, I'm going to have to call you back in half an hour. Hank and I are waiting for an important phone call. Is there an emergency?"

"I wouldn't bloody well call you on Christmas morning if it wasn't. Have you been watching the news?"

"No. What's up?"

"Put him on speaker, Dav," Hank said suddenly, and firmly. There was no disobeying that tone, so Daven hit the speakerphone button and hoped for the best.

"I've got you on speaker. Hank's here. Go ahead."

"Hank, it's Rupe. Listen, one of our double agents was found dead in Colorado. It's all over the news."

Holy mother of...

"Wait," said Hank after a few moments of shocked silence, "was he actually identified as one of our agents?"

Daven felt nearly paralyzed and overwhelmed by anxiety and guilt, until Rupe answered, " *She,* actually. And if they've identified her as a mole, they're not saying it yet."

Despite the fact that he hated himself down to the core for it, Daven found himself incredibly relieved and grateful that the dead agent wasn't his man, but a woman. He would have turned himself in, and Hank would have known his betrayal, and-

"Why is this all over the news?" Hank asked, still reeling and not even thinking to ask who the victim was first.

"Well, because she's one of Colbert's drivers. Found dead with her bike on Seditionists property. And I'm sorry to be the one to tell you this, but it's only a matter of time before they find out what she was doing there. It's been a drop for the past few weeks, and our surveillance video has already been subpoenaed. I think whatever she had was taken by her killer, most likely an Urbane. It could have even been one of us, if they thought she was one of them."

"*Fuck me,*" Hank breathed under his breath. "If this happened at the Greeley office, she was carrying something for me."

"Yep. She's the only agent we have in Colorado right now. Sorry, Hank. Merry Christmas, huh?'

Daven looked at Hank in complete shock; he had not known of any such operation, nor that any of their agents were in Greeley. It was his duty to know absolutely everything.

"What was she carrying?" Dav asked as calmly and disinterestedly as she could.

Hank ignored him. "Thanks, Rupe. It's not even 11am and it already feels like a week since I woke up. How come you called the office, though? Just curious. Dav and I both have our new cell phones on us, and this is the kind of thing they are meant for."

"I did. Yours must be on silent, and his went straight to voicemail like a million times. Listen guys, I'm going to get back to this and get a PR plan together when the inevitable shit hits the fan. Look for an email from me within the next two hours for more details. Call me if you need me...on my cell, of course. That's what it's for, as you said, even though you won't answer it."

Hank pulled his phone out for the first time all morning and dismissed the 17 missed calls from Floyd. "Yeah, mine's on silent. Sorry, we were waiting for a call on Dav's phone. Merry Christmas Rupe, and keep in touch."

Daven seemed frozen in place, so Hank was the one who had to walk around the desk and lean over to hang up the phone.

"Dav," he said gently, "let's call it a day. But first, I'm going to ring the emergency line and see what happens. Maybe our man has been calling all along but your phone's not working."

"Yes, that could be a possibility," Daven blurted as he swept up his phone from the table. "I don't have any missed calls or voicemails, though." He pretended to be flipping through the screens in confusion as he toggled the satellite connection setting back on and prayed for it to connect before Hank could finish dialing from his own phone, which he was busy doing at this very moment.

Hank dialed, paused…hung up, got lost in thought for a few moments, and began dialing again.

"Almost couldn't remember the number. That could be a problem someday. Jesus."

That single slip of memory saved Dav from having an awful lot of explaining to do. In the time it took Hank to re-dial again, and put the phone to his ear, Dav's phone connected to the network and then began ringing.

"Hello?"

"Hey, it's me," Hank said pointlessly, considering they were standing three feet away from each other holding their phones at their ears. "Well, it's working. Maybe it's Rupert's phone, then." He closed his phone.

"That does seem the most logical explanation. I would hate to think we missed the agent's call."

"Dav…you can hang up now, obviously. Maybe it's time to have another espresso, huh? You seem a little shell-shocked."

They both looked at each other quizzically for a few moments, and Daven couldn't help himself from asking the same question that had been previously ignored.

"What was the agent carrying, do you know?"

Hank shrugged. "Depends on the agent. I have a few things in the works."

"Things I didn't know about, you mean?"

"Daven," Hank began in a warning tone, purposely using his full name instead of the nickname to indicate that his patience was nearly at an end. "We've been through this before. We're a *huge* organization. There's things going on with us that even I don't know about, so you shouldn't take it personally. I don't."

"Yes you do, actually."

Hank sighed. "I've said it before, and I'll say it again. You, me, and Rupe together don't possess all the brain power it would require to run this place. If we did, why would we hire anyone else? Do you know how many employees we have right now, besides us?"

Of course he did. "512."

"How many of them do you trust?"

"Seven."

Hank's expression darkened, and he furrowed his eyebrows. "That's....that's not the answer I was looking for. You should have said 512."

"That would be a lie," Daven said simply.

Hank shook his head, and then turned away to gather up all his belongings.

"Time for you to go home, Dav. If our mystery man calls, you have my permission to keep him on the line - in silence - while you race back to the office to verify him. But you're leaving, and so am I."

"Don't forget about Floyd," Daven mumbled. "And take it easy on him. It's Christmas." He was clearly unhappy with his boss right now for several reasons, but Hank didn't have the energy to hold his chief strategist's hand again. They went through this little crisis every once in a while, but it always blew over quickly.

"Yeah, I know. I'm mostly just mad he drove the Thunderbird alone. Damned unsafe."

The three of them walked out together, Floyd perfectly silent as Hank held his arm in an iron grip all the way to the backseat of the car (not the front, which meant he was really in trouble), and drove one behind the other to their respective houses down the street from each other.

Daven was obliged to fight the urge to look at his phone again until he was in the safety and privacy of his home, upon which he sat down at the kitchen table and forced himself to breathe through ninety seconds of calming meditation.

Now...the phone. He was not at all surprised to see 9 voicemails since 8am. Two from Rupe, one from Floyd. Six from an unknown caller. He took a deep breath, cursed himself for being so paranoid, and then dialed into the message center.

CHAPTER FIVE

Bancroft Home

Hank was still furious as he threw the car in park and got out to haul Floyd out of the backseat. His oldest had other ideas about that, though, and quickly emerged from the opposite side of the car. Safe out of his dad's crushing grip.

"Dad, can I-"

"Floyd, it's Christmas day so we're going to put this discussion off until tomorrow. I don't want any apologies right now. In fact, don't say anything. Just get inside."

Floyd stood stock still and looked Hank in the eyes. "I wasn't going to apologize, no matter what you do today or tomorrow. Theo needed you, and you broke your promise."

"So you drove the Thunderbird by yourself and then snuck into my office-"

"And I would do it again," Floyd interrupted calmly, with a dangerously sullen expression. "It's not my fault your phones were off. What if we had a real emergency, dad? Like one of us was dying? Would you even care, then?"

"My phone was on silent for a reason. You have Daven's number, why didn't you call him? He knows never to ignore a call from you."

"I did! Like a million times. It just went straight to voicemail. And you never picked up your office line since you were in his office, and I don't even know his office number so I couldn't call that. This is so unfair, dad. You basically abandoned us. On Christmas day, and I'm going to be the one punished for it?"

Hank said nothing more about the unauthorized drive; Floyd's comments about Daven's phone instantly took precedence. His mind flashed back to what had transpired over the past three hours with the call that never came.

Floyd mistook his dad's sudden silence for penance and strode past him into the house.

Hank didn't even notice. He pulled his phone out of his pocket and dialed the emergency number.

Daven's Townhouse

You have. Nine. New Messages.

First message, 8:01am: "Uh....please tell me you missed my call because you're taking a dump, and not because you're freezing me out. I'll call back in five minutes."

Delete message? 1 for yes, 2 for no. Message deleted.

Message two, 8:07am: "Daven, for god's sake. I called when you told me to, where the hell are you? Are you not picking up because Hank is with you? Get rid of him, we've got to talk."

Delete message? 1 for yes, 2 for no. Message deleted.

Message three, 8:29am: "So this is how you treat your agents, huh? I risk my life for you guys, and you won't even answer my fucking phone call? I'm calling back at 9. You better fucking pick up the phone, Daven. My life is on the line."

Delete message? 1 for yes, 2 for no. Message deleted.

Message four, 8:31am: "Dav, it's Rupe. We've got a bad situation going on. Call me back ASAP."

Delete message? 1 for yes, 2 for no. Message saved.

Message five, 9:00am: "I take it Hank's still with you. Man, if you don't pick up at 9:30 I'm going to...just, pick up the phone!"

Delete message? 1 for yes, 2 for no. Message deleted.

Message six, 9:28am: "Dav, it's Rupe again. I can't reach Hank, guessing he's still out cold from that hangover you wanted him to have. What the hell was that about, anyway? Call me ASAP, our Colorado agent just got zipped. I need to talk to you."

Delete message? 1 for yes, 2 for no. Message deleted.

Message seven, 9:35am: "I'm trying one more time, Daven. If I get zipped before you get the whole story, you've got no one to blame but yourself."

Delete message? 1 for yes, 2 for no. Message deleted.

Message eight, 10:02am: "Uncle Dav, it's Floyd. I'm waiting outside the office to pick dad up. He hasn't called me and Theo needs help. Can you call me right back? If not, I'll come in. I have dad's badge. Thanks."

Delete message? 1 for yes, 2 for no. Message saved.

Message nine, 10:33am: "Fuck you all. I'm calling Rupert. And he's not going to be happy to get this story on top of the other one today. Hope you lose your job like I just lost mine because of our fearless leader's treason. Merry fucking Christmas."

Daven jerked upright and threw down the phone in horror. Shit, had he already called Rupert? Then the phone rang again: the emergency line. Daven blanched, then shakily took a deep breath, said a quick prayer, and hit the answer button.

"Yes?"

"Hey. Long time no talk. It's Hank."

There was a telling pause. "I don't understand. We were just together about 25 minutes ago."

Hank groaned. "I wanted to test this number again. Floyd just told me he's been calling you all morning and your phone wasn't picking up. First thing tomorrow morning I want you and Shane to get on this. Nothing else takes priority, not even the dead woman. We didn't spend hundreds of thousands of dollars on telecommunications infrastructure to be missing calls from agents whose lives are in danger. For all we know, she was calling it, too."

Daven had to fight to remember to breathe again. "I will get on it. First thing tomorrow," he repeated.

"I need you to call around to the field supervisors today and have them check in with our remaining agents, see if anyone else has gone missing."

"Right away. Is Theo alright?"

"I don't know, I haven't gone inside yet. Talk to you later."

Hank hung up and went into the house. Theo was sitting askew on the couch, having cried himself into exhaustion, and Floyd was there with his arm wrapped protectively around his little brother. Hank could not possibly ignore the critically hostile expression his oldest was wearing.

"Floyd," he said sharply, "come with me for a minute. Just want to get this talk over with so we can move on to our Christmas festivities."

"I don't want to talk."

Hank didn't have time for this; he grabbed his son by the arm again and hauled him into the study. Floyd didn't try to struggle, not even when Hank forced him to stand still and look him in the eyes.

"Floyd, I'm only going to say this one time," he said calmly, without rancor. "I shouldn't even be telling you at all, because I don't want you to have dangerous information. There was a woman found dead in Colorado this morning on Seditionists property."

Floyd swallowed hard. "I heard that on the radio station in the car. One of Colbert's assistants."

"His driver, specifically. She was a double agent. For me. That's why I got stuck at the office, okay? That, and one other thing going on that Daven is handling. If I could have gotten away sooner, I would have. We were actually on the way out when you showed up. I did *not* forget it was Christmas. Do you understand?" His tone was very gentle now, and indeed, he was feeling extremely sorry for manhandling one of his children (twice) on Christmas day.

Floyd nodded, expression already less angry. "So...you're going to be working all day, then?"

"No. Rupe is handling this one. I'm only angry about you driving the Thunderbird by yourself. You have a driver's permit that allows you behind the wheel if - and *only* if - an adult is with you. You could have been stopped by the cops and arrested."

"But it was only-"

"Our drivers literally live fifty feet from where we're standing, and I've instructed you a hundred times to use them if something like this happens. You did when Theo broke his wrist, and when the dog needed to go to the vet. There was no excuse for this today, Floyd. None. I know you care about your brother, but you have to keep your head on your shoulders and think straight in times of crisis. I'm very disappointed with you right now."

Ouch. Floyd didn't have an answer for that.....what possible defense *could* he have?

"Okay, dad. I'm sorry," Floyd mumbled contritely. He really was, too.

"I can see that you are. You're forgiven, but I'll still have to punish you tomorrow."

"How?"

"What do *you* think?"

Floyd swallowed hard, then said quietly, "It's so much worse waiting, can't we just do it now? Theody's asleep."

"No," Hank replied firmly. "It's Christmas. Pull yourself together and then come out to open your presents."

Hank left the study and went to pour himself a long overdue glass of whiskey.

"Rupe, it's Dav."

"For the hundredth time, I know. That's what caller ID is for. What's up?"

"An agent called through on the emergency line yesterday and then tried to call it back again this morning. For whatever reason, it didn't forward to my phone. He said he's going to call you, so I was just wondering if you had heard from him."

"But...if it didn't go through, how do you know he's going to call me?"

Shit. "Well, the call itself didn't come through, but the voicemail did. Eventually. I just got it now."

There was a long pause while Rupert moved away from the sound of Christmas festivities, and the other line became progressively quieter until there was no sound at all.

"Rupe? You there?"

 "Yeah, I'm here. And yes, I got his call about half an hour ago. You and I need to talk."

"I know. When?"

"Now. You said that your phone wasn't working this morning, which I find really strange. The technology has proven to be extremely reliable."

Daven swallowed hard. "Yeah, I know. Hank wants me to get on it in the morning with Shane. Maybe it was-"

"Dav, *stop*. I know you were hiding this agent's calls. Blocking them, because you were with Hank. That explains why my calls to you didn't go through, either. For hours."

There was nothing to say. Visions of packing up office boxes and being disgracefully escorted out of the building suddenly filled Daven's vivid imagination. Ten years of friendship with Hank and Rupe, and countless hours of hard work with the Seditionists. Wasted.

"If you really did talk to the agent," Dav eventually replied, very slowly, "then you'll know why I did that. But...if you and Hank want my resignation, you can have it today."

Rupe sighed. "Yeah, and I'd be next in line behind you for talking with an unverified asset. This stays between us. What did you think of this agent's claims?"

That change of tack threw Daven for a loop, and he took his phone away from his ear, stared at it quizzically, and then put it back.

"I...I...there's no reason not to look into them. Except that it feels so wrong doing it without Hank."

"You'll have to get over that. This isn't an emotional or subjective decision, Dav. We have to do it. You should know that from the start. To be honest, I'm disappointed you didn't come to me yesterday and tell me this was going on. I could have diverted the calls to my phone and talked to the guy while you waited at the office. At least now I know why you used me to get Hank drunk. This is just shameful all around."

Rupe was clearly angry now, and Dav had to work hard to put that fire out. Fast.

"You're right," he said contritely. "I'm sorry. I shouldn't have condescended to subterfuge."

"No, you shouldn't have, and if you ever do it again I'll turn you in to Hank myself. Now, moving on. Can you talk about 9pm tonight? My family should be asleep by then."

"Yes."

"Good. Talk to you then."

Click

CHAPTER SIX

Floyd was still sulking after dinner despite a couple of impromptu swats to his rear that Hank had administered in the early afternoon for an attitude adjustment. It surprisingly hadn't worked, but at least Theo had been significantly cheered by the quality and quantity of his Christmas presents. It even appeared he had forgotten all about this morning's drama, which irritated Floyd to no end, because now Theo got off scot-free and Floyd was going to be the one suffering tomorrow morning for his brother's tantrums.

"Floyd," Hank called from behind his giant mug as his oldest went around collecting all the discarded wrapping paper and angrily stuffing it into the trash compactor. Theody was already asleep, of course, and didn't have to help. As usual. The kid knew how to get out of his chores.

"Yes, sir?" Floyd replied automatically.

"Did you like your Christmas presents? You haven't said much. Hope you aren't disappointed. Theo seemed to be hurt you weren't excited about the video games he gave you."

"Because they're stupid, and I already had two of them. His lazy ass didn't even bother to check."

Hank was the one who had picked out the games, so Floyd's rude comments were officially the last straw for the day.

"Alright. That's enough. Get in your pajamas and go to the spare room. When I'm done with my coffee, we're going to have a chat. Leave your phone with me."

Floyd stopped what he was doing to hand his dad his phone, then he turned away and rolled his eyes as he trudged upstairs to change.

The 10x10 "spare room" with its bright white walls, white tile floor, and little twin bed pushed into the corner was seriously disliked by the brothers, and usually the threat of being sent there for a few hours was enough to straighten them up. The windows were still frosted due to its former life as a kitchen pantry, and the room was constantly cold due to a problem with the heating unit that had yet to be resolved. But worse than that, it was horribly, incredibly boring. And it made a person think too much. Floyd had nicknamed it "the asylum."

Hank knew full well that sending his boys to their own rooms was the farthest thing from a punishment that he could possibly dream up, so this was the next best thing. He hated having to do it to Floyd on Christmas night, but there was no choice now. The boy needed to settle down and re-center himself.

Hank suspected that Sunday was going to be a colossal headache on many fronts.

"Rupe, it's Daven."

"Yes. *I know* . Caller ID. Remember?"

"It's nine o'clock."

"I know that, too. *Clock*. Remember?"

Daven grunted. "I'm not looking forward to this conversation but it has to be done. But first we have to address one thing. This man is not verified, and we should do that first.

"Agreed. The problem is, he wouldn't give me his code."

Daven paused. "Why not? That's incredibly suspicious."

"Not really. He's never met me and doesn't trust me. Said he would only give it to you directly. You're going to have to talk to him, Dav. There's no avoiding it."

"Didn't you tell him we won't look into his claims until he's verified?"

Rupe sighed. "Actually, he says you promised to look them immediately before he would even tell you the thing about Hank. And he's holding you to it. Did you really say that?"

Dav's mind flashed back to his very first conversation with the agent, at Hank's house during the Christmas party. *Shit*. He definitely had said that. His heart was pounding suddenly.

"What else did he tell you, Rupe? Start from the very beginning. Don't leave anything out, just tell me exactly. Every word."

Rupert pinched the bridge of his nose and took another drink of wine. This was turning out to be quite the nightmare of a day.

"Alright. It wasn't much, but brace yourself…"

Floyd was pretending to be asleep, back to the door, when his dad showed up for "the talk."

Hank didn't buy it. "Sit up, Floyd."

Floyd ignored him, so Hank sat next to him on the bed and gently pulled him upright. He wasn't ready to fight right now, or ever. He wanted to forget this was happening and go to bed. But it had been a long time since Floyd needed *a talk,* and he was really pushing Hank's buttons lately.

"Look," he said, running his hand through his son's perfectly cut hair. "I know it's been a rough day. I just want to say Merry Christmas to you one more time, and see if we can end tonight on a good note. I'll let you go back to your bedroom if you just talk to me for five minutes. *Talk.* Not argue. Okay? Look at me, Floyd."

Floyd didn't look, but at least he responded at all. "Doesn't matter where I am, I'm not going to be able to sleep knowing what's going to happen in the morning."

Hank swallowed hard; he had already been harboring a ton of guilt about that same pending event. But it had to be done; Floyd had put himself in a terrible and risky position by driving the Thunderbird almost 20 miles without a license. Not to mention risking the incredible media circus that would have ensued afterwards by the arrest of a party leader's son.

He needed to tread carefully, so he said gently, "Losing sleep over it isn't going to help matters."

"Do it at midnight, then, so it's technically not on Christmas day. That's only three hours away, I should survive until then."

Hank sighed to himself. "No. But…Floyd, look at me. I mean it."

When Floyd looked up, finally - eyes wet with unshed tears - Hank lost his anger immediately, exactly as he expected. The boy was a master at disarming his father, and they both knew it.

"On Monday, I promise we will go to the DMV and you can test for your provisional license. If you pass, that means you can drive alone, but with no passengers. Not even Theody."

Floyd looked away, starting to sniff. "I don't think they'll be able to get me in so soon."

Hank smiled. "Well, let's just say I have a little bit of influence there. We'll get you an appointment. Whether or not you pass is completely in your hands, though. Tomorrow afternoon we'll go driving around for a bit after church, ok? As long as it takes until you feel ready to kill it on Monday."

"Dad…" Floyd began, a bit miserably, so low that Hank almost didn't hear him.

"Keep talking, Floyd. We're not at five minutes yet."

"You're not going to like what I want to say, though."

Hank smiled encouragingly. "Well, you haven't liked anything I've said so far. Seems only fair you should be allowed to return the favor. I'll even let you cuss, if you feel like it. But no name-calling."

Floyd shrugged. "Fine. I think…it was really shitty what you did today. You broke your promise to Theo. And to me, too, but I didn't care as much as he did. You should have heard him crying, dad. I just…I did what I had to do. I'm not trying to get out of anything for driving the car alone, but I want to let you know that nothing is ever going to make me sorry for being mad at you for being a crappy father."

"Floyd-"

Floyd's volume and temper escalated. "We woke up to an empty house. By ourselves. On *Christmas morning.* You could have left us a note to tell us there was an emergency so that Theo didn't freak out. This was the worst Christmas ever and I just wanted it to be over from the moment it started. Maybe you could buy Theo's forgiveness with expensive presents, but you'll never buy mine. Not for this, or for anything else."

Jesus, thought Hank with a bit of wry amusement. *Be careful what you ask for.*

The tears were falling profusely now, but Floyd did not sniffle or wipe them away. They just trickled down as silent witnesses to the young boy's grief. Hank didn't respond right away; he needed time to collect his wits again. He had no idea of the depth of Floyd's resentment for him until now…and it stung. Hard.

In a gentle but firm voice he responded, "Alright, I think I get the picture. And I'm going to make a deal with you. Are you calm enough to talk to me reasonably right now?"

"I don't know," Floyd sniffed.

"Okay. Well, this is what I'm going to propose. I promise you I will always, *always,* let you know when I'm leaving and when I'll be back, and I'll let you know if I'm running late. My purpose for keeping you in the dark in the past has been to protect you. Obviously, that backfired today. I'm also going to give you Daven's office number, and Rupert's two numbers, so that you can reach them in an emergency. I'll make sure to reinforce that they must pick up if you call, so you have to be careful not to use it unless there is a dire emergency and you can't reach me. Okay?"

Floyd nodded silently, still unhappy. "In exchange for what?"

"Never repeating what happened this morning. You know that Daven had a gun pointed at you because we thought you were a burglar?"

"Yes." Floyd shuddered at the memory.

"Floyd, I'm only going to say this once - and I mean it. That's the second time you've shown up at the office without my permission. There will not be a third. You're not to come within a mile of it ever again, unless I take you there myself. If you do, I'm sending you and Theo to boarding school again to keep you safe. This is not negotiable. Do we understand each other?"

Floyd nodded as he wiped his eyes, and they solemnly shook hands to seal the deal. He wasn't upset by the thought of boarding school, considering he'd actually liked it. They had spent three months there while Hank was busy traveling for his re-election campaign last year. Floyd had made friends and been popular. He'd even thought of asking to be sent back...until he remembered that Theo still might never recover from the trauma of being bullied by his own roommates.

"Okay, that part's settled, then," said Hank with finality as he stood up abruptly. "Now for the rest of it. The driving infraction. Since we've talked, and I know how wound up you are about waiting, this crappy father is willing to honor your request to get it over with now if you still want to. You need to sleep tonight, big day tomorrow. But it's up to you."

Floyd hesitated, then carefully slid down onto his knees and bent over the bed. Hank took off his belt with trembling hands.

He *really* didn't want to do this.

Especially because he knew Floyd was exactly right.

CHAPTER SEVEN

Hank had a hell of a time waking Floyd up on Sunday for church. Out of the three of them, only Theo was eager to go, as usual. He shuffled impatiently from foot to foot at the door of Floyd's room while their father poked and prodded at the grumpy teenager.

"*Floyd* . UP. Now. Or else we're going to cancel that driving lesson I promised you, and no appointment tomorrow."

"Don't care," Floyd mumbled. "Go without me."

Theo braced himself, grinning with expectation. He knew exactly what was going to happen next. Hell, everyone did. Even Floyd.

"Ow! Dad, stop," Floyd cried as Hank pulled him bodily out of bed and dumped him onto the floor, all the while unwrapping him from the blanket which was quickly tossed aside. There was no anger or manhandling in the action, just the usual impatient purposefulness. The spectacle was practically a weekly ritual at this point.

Hank was perfectly calm, although much shorter on temper than usual. "If you're not ready and waiting at the door in twenty minutes, my belt is coming back off when we return. Your choice, buddy."

Belt?

Back off?

Theo ghosted out the doorway and quietly ran down the stairs, all trace of amusement gone. He waited in the kitchen, rigid as a statue, shaking a little while his brother and father made themselves presentable. Despite his lack of sympathy for Floyd's inability to get out of bed without being harassed into it, he really hated it when his brother pushed dad far enough to actually be punished. And it was taking less and less these days for that to happen.

Hank and Floyd Bancroft were far more different than alike, but they did share a strong opinion that church was a colossal waste of time. Keeping up the appearance of being a religious family was necessary to his position as leader of the Seditionists, however, the party having more deeply spiritual constituents and leaders than the Urbanes. Daven and Rupert were well-known for being highly devout and vocal about their beliefs, and a couple of years ago they had an enormous fight with Hank at the office because the party was getting bad press about having leaders who couldn't agree on simple religious matters. It wasn't true, of course, but appearances were everything. So after that fight, Hank gave in and went to church.

The press, of course, quickly dropped the story and let them be...as long as he went every Sunday, that is. And he knew they were waiting for him to slip up, watching from their tinted cars across the street. Even being late for services would have caused incredible drama, which was why he was so hard on Floyd every Sunday morning even though he desperately wanted to sleep in, too. 7am services were brutal, even more so on an empty stomach. But that was what their "faith" demanded.

Hank hated the press and church in equal measure.

As usual, when they entered the church Hank turned and waved pointedly at the press cars like he was grand marshal of a parade, plastering a disgustingly wide smile on his face. Watching from inside, Daven sighed and cringed.

"Must you do that every time, Hank?" he muttered in annoyance as he and his boss took their usual pew in the back row.

Hank smiled, but did not look at Daven. "Yep. Just want to make sure they know I'm here. That it's really me, and not some doppelganger. Wouldn't want to cause another media circus, now would I?"

"They know it's you. You're just mocking them at this point," Daven grumbled.

"Not sorry, Dav. Get used to it."

Hank sighed and leaned back against the wall (the very existence of it being why he preferred the back row, although he insisted it was for security purposes). He wanted to close his eyes so badly and take a nap, but Daven would rightly kill him for that. He chuckled to himself at the thought, then picked up on some kind of general disturbance in the crowd. *Oh god.* His sons were seating themselves up in the side balcony, shoving each other for space and bickering loudly. Everyone below was staring at them, then back at Hank, then up again at the boys. The service was moments away from starting, so Hank couldn't exactly get up to go talk to them.

He kept his cool and turned to speak directly into Dav's ear. "Ask a guard to calm the boys down, please." *Before I kill them*, he added to himself as he looked around the congregation with a slightly humorous apologetic expression.

"Already done," Daven whispered back, having noticed the situation long before Hank did and quietly summoning help from the guards with the radio microphone inside his suit lapel. Avery slipped into the scene to whisper something to the boys, who stilled immediately and dared not look anywhere but at the altar. Hank was immensely satisfied by that, returned Avery's eye contact with a smile and nod, and turned his mind to other things. By the time the sermon started it was already forgotten in favor of worrying some more about the telecommunications problem at the office.

The boys sat rigid in their pews, determined not to make another sound. Like his father, Floyd also immediately tuned out of the sermon and began thinking about other things, like last year when he and Theo slipped away from their guards and hailed a cab bound for Disneyland. The cab driver had recognized them, however, and quickly turned around and delivered them to the bewildered receptionist at Seditionist HQ. Dad was out of town, so Rupert took them home after immediately firing the driver and guards who had been in charge of watching them. He then hired the cabbie to replace the driver, so the man was now enjoying a lucrative salary and had quickly become a favorite amongst the women on the household staff.

Suffice to say, Floyd and Theo learned an unforgettable lesson during the whole affair, both emotionally and physically, and now they obeyed the new guards better than they obeyed their father...a fact which had thoroughly annoyed Hank until he realized he could use it to his advantage, and then it amused him. Avery in particular had absolutely no qualms about stepping in to prevent an escalation, so Hank was glad he had been closest.

Hank himself also obeyed his own assigned guards down to the letter; after all, they were there to ensure his safety at the cost of their own lives. There was no one who respected the black-suited men more than Hank Bancroft, and they respected him in return and took good care of him and his sons.

The sermon dragged on. And on. And on. Daven glanced at the suddenly still man next to him, saw what he was doing between his legs, and resisted the urge to curse. He leaned over to his boss.

"Seriously? Put the phone away."

"Shhhhhh. I'm praying," hissed Hank as he kept his head down and continued to scroll through his emails.

"Hank. Stop."

After waiting in vain for a few long moments, Daven reached over and snatched the phone away, dropping it into his opposite pocket and then folding his hands again in his lap. Hank looked at him aghast, with a dangerous expression he very rarely wore.

"Give it back."

Daven looked straight ahead and didn't move. "No."

"Give. It. Back."

"*No*. Pay attention to the sermon, Hank."

Hank straightened up and looked ahead, feeling like a chastised little child. After pouting for a few moments, he glanced aside to the balcony and caught Floyd and Theo watching him, laughing behind their hands, having clearly seen what Daven had just done. *Shit. So much for setting a good example.*

He gave them a stern warning glance, placing a finger to his lips in a "shushing" gesture.

Then he couldn't help but laugh, too.

Daven rolled his eyes and sunk deeper back into the pew.